THE MYSTICAL
ROSE OF TEPEYAC

This is the story of the miraculous apparitions of Our Lady of Guadalupe in 1531 to a humble Nahuan named Juan Diego on the hill of Tepeyac, Mexico.

Cora Hussey

The Mystical Rose of Tepeyac

Cora Hussey

First Edition
Copyright © 1997 by Cora Hussey

For information write to: Cora Hussey, P.O. Box 320653, San Francisco, CA 94132-0653.

Library of Congress Catalog Card Number: 97-94846

Printed in San Francisco, California, USA December 1997 - Published by the Author.

ISBN 0-9661830-0-2

Cover Design by Cora Hussey

To the loving memory
of my Dad,
forever in my heart.

ACKNOWLEDGMENTS

WITH GREAT APPRECIATION AND DEEP GRATITUDE TO:

His Excellency, Most Rev. Norberto Rivera Carrera, Archbishop of Mexico, for graciously allowing me to use the copy of Miguel Cabrera's painting "The Miracle of Guadalupe."

Ms. Dolores Massiah, Licensing Coordinator at Corbis-Bettman, for her generosity in granting permission to reproduce the photo of the Somalia Boy in my booklet.

Mr. Daniel J. Slive, Coordinator of Bibliographic Services, and Ms. Susan Danforth, Assistant Librarian at The John Brown Carter Library, for permitting me to use a copy of the 17th century engraving of Juan Diego.

Dr. Michael Marmor, Chairman Department of Ophthalmology, Stanford Medical Center, for his advice and assistance with the Purkinje-Sanson reflections.

Stanford University Green Library's history and rare books collection staff, for their hospitality, courtesy, and invaluable help throughout my many weeks of research.

Ms. Heidi Heilemann and Ms. Janet Morrison of the Lane Medical Library at Stanford, for their patience, indulgence, and all their help.

And my special thanks to Dr. Steven G. Kramer, Professor and Chairman, Department of Ophthalmology at University of California, San Francisco, and Director of Beckman Vision Center, for graciously explaining to me the reflections in the human eye.

PROLOGUE

This short story is a loving tribute honoring Our Lady of Guadalupe for having restored my health when I was dying of poisoning in 1994. It commemorates her apparitions to a humble Nahuan named Juan Diego on the hill of Tepeyac in 1531. Reprinted in this booklet is the story of my mysterious illness and instantaneous healing.

Our Lady is a loving and merciful Mother, who hears our laments and consoles us. Her supreme promise to Juan Diego is an everlasting pledge of love to those who seek her help and protection.

Many writers have translated the Nican Mopohua from Nahuatl to Spanish, and from Spanish to English. It was written in Nahuatl by the Aztec scholar Antonio Valeriano shortly before the death of Juan Diego in 1548.

Although my narrative account of the miracle of Guadalupe was inspired by the Nican Mopohua, meaning "Here It Is Told," I did not translate it verbatim. Instead, I used my own style and voice.

The diminutive form of salutation between Our Lady and Juan Diego is customarily practiced by the people of Mexico and Latin America. It denotes respect and affection, and is an intimate way of greeting loved ones, especially when talking to children.

Cora Hussey

PREFACE

My inspiration to write about the apparitions of Our Lady of Guadalupe came to me in the summer of 1996.

In my twenties, I had the honor and the pleasure of meeting Our Lady for the first time during a visit to relatives in Mexico City. At that time one could look at Her Sacred Image from a short distance. When we look at Her portrait, our vision is magnetized by Her compassionate eyes. Her gaze illuminates our hearts with Her Presence and Her Love, and our wishes are to lose ourselves forever in the wonder of those mysterious and beautiful eyes.

Personally, I did not know much about the history of Guadalupe; I only knew of Her miraculous healing powers. After my instantaneous healing in 1994, I felt indebted to Her, and wanted to express my gratitude by doing something special for Her. My inner voice said: "Proclaim your cure; She gave you back your life, write about Her miraculous apparitions to Juan Diego at Tepeyac. Introduce Her to people who, like you, are not well acquainted with the 1531 Guadalupan event." That was a big order for someone like me, who has very little time for writing, much less do research. Nevertheless, the thought was implanted in my mind, and I toyed with the idea until one day in October 1996, when I suffered from amnesia for several hours. All my hospital tests were negative. And as in 1994, my husband Bern and I gave thanks to Our Lady for having restored my health. My thirst for knowledge about Her apparitions was somewhat quenched when I began doing research. There is so much literature about Our Lady of Guadalupe that I would never finish reading in one lifetime everything that has been written since She appeared to Juan Diego on the hillock of Tepeyac.

Besides getting to know Her better, something beautiful has happened to me. I no longer feel timid about my grammar, nor afraid to express my thoughts and the deepest feelings of my heart. My Lady, my Queen, and dearest Child, has paved the rough path, taking me by the hand, guiding me, and showing me the way to a happier and more fulfilling life.

To me, She is not just an Image in a painting. To me, She is real! She embraces my pain and my sorrow. She sustains me, consoles me, and uplifts my spirits. She is a rainbow of hope, peace and joy. She is truly a Merciful Mother to those who trust Her, seek Her help, and above all, to those who love Her. All we need to do is ask Her!

Blessings,
Cora Hussey

TABLE OF CONTENTS

ILLUSTRATIONS

DEFINITION OF NAHUATL AND SPANISH WORDS:

Mazeuhalli: A member of the lowest class in the Aztec Empire.

Huei Tlamahuicoltica: "She Marvelously Appeared."

Tilma: A blanket or cape.

Ayate: Cloth made of fibers from the maguey cactus.

The clothing worn by the Mazeuhallis

"AN OUTSTANDING MIRACLE HAS TAKEN PLACE" (Acts 4:16).

This booklet is for those of unwavering faith, who do not need proof in order to believe. "He who doubts is like a wave driven by the sea." (Jas. 1:6).

Many scientists, eminent historians, and fine artists have concluded that the miracle of Guadalupe could not be other than a supernatural phenomenon. "If you do not believe me, believe the works." (John 10:38, 14:11). For those who believe, no explanation is necessary; nevertheless, we have mounting evidence attesting to the divine nature of Our Lady's portrait. The results of the extensive scientific analyses of the tilma have been compiled in an encyclopedia of relevant data about the miracle at Tepeyac. Therefore, I believe that the painting on Juan Diego's tilma could not possibly have been made by human hands.

I am neither a prophet nor a psychic, but this I know: during my near-death experience in 1994, Our Lady gave me a glimpse of Her beautiful presence: a transcendent moment that I will never forget. Her glorious vision has been deeply etched in my memory forever! There is not a molecule of doubt in me. My miraculous healing was instantaneous. She not only cured me, but She also changed my life. I have been blessed with a profound and powerful faith.

"I am a Merciful Mother . . ."

2

THE MYSTICAL ROSE OF TEPEYAC

This is the story of the miraculous apparitions of Our Lady of Guadalupe to a humble Nahuan named Juan Diego, at Tepeyac. It happened ten years after Cortes had conquered Mexico.

The First Apparition

On Saturday, December 9, 1531, dawn was breaking on the misty hillock of Tepeyac. The earth was peaceful and calm on this bitterly cold and hushed morning, as a humble 57-year-old Nahuan named Juan Diego hurried on his way to hear Mass at the Franciscan Mission in Tenochtitlan (now known as Mexico City). He was lean and fairly tall, with a shaggy mane of black hair, a meager goatee, and a cat-whisker mustache. His rugged weathered skin was the color of burnt umber, and his language was Nahuatl. Although he was getting on in years, he was still nimble as a deer. Every Saturday and Sunday morning, he walked the familiar nine miles to the church of Tlatelolco in Tenochitlan, at a jaunty pace, swiftly treading along the curvy, narrow and rocky paths. He walked on bare feet, wearing only a breech-cloth and a tilma, as was the custom of the Mazeuhallis. His tilma was as stiff as buckram, and it did not give enough protection for the raw winter weather. His cape was made of a coarse cloth, woven of maguey cactus. It consisted of two pieces approximately eighteen inches wide by six feet long, which were stitched together with a flimsy maguey thread using needles made from the thorns of the plant. Sandals and cotton were only for the upper class of the Aztecs.

As he approached the foot of the hill, a beautiful, sweet music emanated from the cloud-capped hilltop, as though a choir of angels and melodious birds were singing to celebrate the dawn of a new day. He stopped to listen to the soft and delightful singing

3

of the birds which surpassed the mellifluous singing of the bellbird, and that of the colorful trogon. The enchanting concert enraptured him. When the singing ceased momentarily at intervals, the hills reverberated with their joyous hymn. Juan Diego stood transfixed as a dazzling light burst forth from the crest of the hill. He looked up to where the sun rises, and saw a shining cloud blazing with a grand display of colors. He was trembling - not so much from the freezing weather, as from supernatural awe. He said to himself, "Am I worthy of what I see and what I hear? Am I dreaming? Where am I? Am I in heaven?" Suddenly, an ominous silence fell on the valley and held time still. Then, from the brilliant cloud whence the celestial singing had come, there emerged the tender voice of a girl, affectionately calling his name: **"Juanito, Juan Dieguito."** His fears melted into joy as he rapidly climbed the rock-studded hill to see who was calling him. As he reached the top, the bright, ethereal cloud evaporated into a luminous mist, revealing the resplendent, heavenly apparition. Behold, standing in the bright mist in great glory and majesty was a maiden of marvelous beauty. She had dark skin and angelic features, and she wore a long-sleeved rose-petal tunic trimmed in ermine at the cuffs and embossed with a delicate, golden, floral design. Her ebony hair was parted in the middle and covered with a long, turquoise veil trimmed in gold and decorated with golden stars. The hillock on which she stood glittered like precious jewels. The mesquites, nopales and all the brittle prickly plants surrounding the cliff were shining like gold. The ground appeared to be covered with a blanket of twinkling emeralds and turquoise, dazzling like iridescent prisms in a spectrum of colors. Her entire image was framed with golden rays of light, blazing like the sun. The brilliance of her garments sparkled like diamonds. Juan Diego was awestricken. Smiling, she beckoned him to approach her. When he was in her immediate presence, he marveled at her regal grandeur. Bowing with reverence, he heard her amiable, courteous, and loving words in his native Nahuatl: **"Listen Juanito, the least of my sons, where are you going?**

4

Looking up into her radiant face and compassionate eyes, he replied, "My Lady, My Queen, and my little Girl, I am on my way to the church of Santiago in Tlatilolco, to hear mass and the teachings of the priests, the apostolic delegates of our Lord and Savior."

She then revealed to Juan Diego Her identity and Her supreme wish. **"Know for sure, my dearest son, that I am the Ever Virgin, Holy Mary, Mother of the True God. The Creator of Mankind, of Heaven and Earth, and present everywhere."** After hearing Her sacred words, Juan Diego knelt at Her feet and bowed. Our Lady blessed him, and told him, **"I have an important errand to entrust to you, the least of my sons. In order to accomplish all that my merciful and compassionate heart promises, it is my wish that you go to the palace where the Bishop of Mexico lives, and tell him that I sent you. Manifest to him my great desire to have a temple built in my honor, here, in this llano, where I stand, so that all those who pray here will bear witness to my love, my compassion, my help and my protection. For I am a merciful mother to you and to all those who love me, and trust me, and invoke my help. I will listen to their laments, and will console and remedy their sorrow, their pain and their suffering."** Juan Diego was enthralled by Her marvelous words, which sounded like a beautiful poem. Sensing his dread of Her imposing message, Our Lady gave him a look eloquent with compassion. Smiling, She gestured him to stand up and said to him in a sweet tone of voice, **"Don't be afraid, my little son. Just tell the Bishop, precisely, all that you have seen, heard, marveled at, and admired. Be assured that I shall be grateful. I will glorify you. I shall honor and bless you and make you happy. You will deserve my recompense for your work and hardship in doing my bidding. Now that you have heard my orders, the least of my sons, go and make your utmost efforts."**

Her warm and comforting words appeased him. Taking a deep breath, he bowed before Her again, and promised, "My most noble Lady, and my dearest Child, your little Indian is going right away to fulfill your orders. Your humble servant bids you good-day." He left Her and descended the hill, taking the causeway that led straight to Tenochtitlan.

Juan Diego did not hear mass that day, because for him, Our Lady's mission was top priority. When he reached the city, he went directly to the palace of Fray Juan de Zumarraga, a Franciscan who had disembarked from Spain in 1528 to become the first Bishop of Mexico. As soon as Juan Diego arrived, he begged the Bishop's steward to announce him, but the household servants were inattentive and arrogant with the lower class. They made Juan Diego wait for hours. After all, to them he was just a nobody. But because of his enduring patience and persistence, the steward finally allowed him to see the Bishop. Kneeling before the prelate, Juan Diego related through an interpreter every word that the Queen of Heaven had said to him. He told him that at dawn on the hillock of Tepeyac, he had seen and spoken with the Mother of God. She had said that it was Her wish that a temple be built on the hill, where She had appeared to him. The Bishop was reluctant to believe Juan Diego, and sent him away saying, "My son, I would like for you to come back again some other time, when I will calmly hear your story from the beginning. At that time, I will seriously consider your wishes and the reason for which you have come to see me."

Second Apparition

After having spent all day waiting to see the Bishop, Juan Diego left the palace disappointed and brokenhearted, and headed back to Tepeyac to look for the Mother of God. It was twilight when he reached the little hill where he had first seen Her. She was waiting for him. When Juan Diego saw Her, he went to Her, and dropped to his knees. With great sadness he conveyed to Her his failure to convince the Bishop. "My dearest Child, my Queen and my Lady, I did exactly as you asked me. I obeyed your orders, and went where you sent me to deliver your kind and spirited words. Although it was difficult, and I waited for a long time to see the Bishop, I finally delivered your message. His Excellency was kind and attentive, but he did not believe me. He thinks that the story about the house that you wish to have built here is not from your lips, but mine. He told me to come back at another time, when he could see me at leisure. I beg you, my Lady, and my little Child, to send a more respectable messenger so that the Bishop will believe your amiable words. I am just a common and humble little man: a nobody. It is not my place to go where you have sent me. You need someone prominent and prestigious to deliver your message to his Eminence, so that he will believe. Please forgive me, my Queen. Don't be angry with me, my Mistress, for distressing your heart. I am sorry if I have upset you."

With great compassion, understanding, and gentleness, the Most Holy Virgin replied, **"Listen, my dearest son, and know for certain that I have many messengers whom I could send to deliver my word and carry out my will. But it is necessary that you, personally, go and plead earnestly to the Bishop, so that through your intercession my wish and my will shall be fulfilled. I command you, my dearest Juanito, to go again tomorrow to see the Bishop, and tell him that it is my will that he build my temple. Please tell him that it is the Virgin Mary, Mother of the true God, who sends you."**

"I am sorry, my Lady and my Queen, to have caused you anxiety and displeasure. Please be assured that I will deliver your message again tomorrow morning, and that I will do my best to convince the Bishop. Perhaps I will not be heard. If I am heard, I might not be believed. Nevertheless, tomorrow at sunset I will come back with his answer. With your permission, my Lady and my Child, I respectfully leave you for now. I wish you a restful and peaceful night." He then went home to Tlatelolco.

On Sunday, December 10th, after Mass, Juan Diego went back to the Bishop's home to deliver the Virgin's message. After much difficulty and a long wait, he finally got an audience in the afternoon. Juan Diego bowed, and in tears he told the Bishop about his second meeting with the Mother of God. "The Heavenly Queen asked me to come again to deliver Her message, your Excellency."

The Bishop asked Juan Diego many questions: "Exactly where have you seen her? What does she look like? Does she move around?"

"My dear sir, I see Her and meet with Her exactly where I have been telling you: on the little hill of Tepeyac, where I first saw Her. She is a maiden of glorious beauty. Her skin is the same color as mine, and there is an aura of supernatural splendor about Her. A bursting cloud of light radiates from Her garments. She smiles, and moves about ever so naturally." The Bishop was still full of doubts, and told Juan Diego that if his Lady was who she claimed to be, she should send him a sign.

"What kind of a sign?" Juan Diego asked him.

"Any sign," replied the Bishop, and sent Juan Diego away, ordering two of his most trusted servants to follow him: "Find out where he goes and with whom he talks."

Defeated, Juan Diego left the palace. The Bishop's men trailed closely behind Juan Diego until he reached the rocky ravine near Tepeyac, but he disappeared near the little wooden bridge that spanned the gorge at the foot of the hill. They became confused and disoriented, and lost sight of him. The men looked for Juan Diego everywhere, but could not find him. Then they returned to the palace, and told the Bishop that Juan Diego had lied to him. The servants warned the priest that they thought the Mazeuhalli was also a sorcerer, because he had disappeared before their eyes. The two men plotted that if he ever came back, they would capture him and punish him severely, so that he would never tell lies again.

Third Apparition

Meanwhile, before sunset Juan Diego returned to Tepeyac and climbed to the hilltop, where the beautiful Lady was waiting for him. With great sadness in his heart, he apologized again for his failure to convince the bishop. He told Her that the Bishop had asked him for a sign. The Lady thanked him and told him, **"So be it, my little son. Come back tomorrow for my sign that you will take to the Bishop. He will then believe you, and no longer be suspicious, or have any more doubts of what you tell him. Go home and rest, now. I'll be here, waiting for you tomorrow."**

Juan Diego respectfully bowed, wishing Her a pleasant evening, and went home to Tolpetlac, to the house that he had built near the home of his uncle, Juan Bernardino. He had lived there for the two years since the death of his wife, Maria Lucia. When he arrived at home, he found his uncle gravely ill with the plague. Therefore, Juan Diego did not return to Tepeyac for the sign the next day as he had promised. His uncle had a high fever, and his condition worsened. The healer came to see him, but there was not much he could do; Juan Bernardino was gravely ill. When nightfall came, he begged his nephew to go to the church of Tlatelolco before daybreak and bring a priest to give him the last rites.

Fourth Apparition

At dawn on Tuesday, December 12th, Juan Diego rushed to Tenochitlan to fetch the priest for his dying uncle. When he reached the west side of the hill, where the sun sets and where the causeway to the city begins, Juan Diego said to himself: "If I take this road, which is my usual shortcut, perhaps the Lady will see me and will detain me so that I can take Her sign to the Bishop. First, I have to take care of my own problems and bring a priest to my uncle, who is waiting." Therefore, in order to avoid meeting the

Lady and losing time, he decided to take the eastern course, cutting around the hill. "This way," he thought, "the Queen of Heaven will not see me and will not detain me."

He felt guilty for having to deceive the Mother of God in this manner, but he had no choice. However, She, who knows and sees everything, had been watching him all the time. As he emerged on the other side of the hill, he was greatly surprised to see the Lady descending to meet him. She stopped on the side of the road and asked him, **"Juanito, why are you avoiding me? What's the matter, my dear son? Where are you going?"**

Nervous, and overwhelmed with shame and remorse, he dropped to his knees. Removing his hat, he bowed. Then, trying to conceal his guilt and grief, he smiled and greeted Her jovially, "My young Lady, the smallest of my Daughters, my Child, how are you this morning? I hope that you are well and happy." But Juan Diego knew that this was not a time for lively talk and congeniality. He became somber and sad again, and with great sorrow he told Her that his uncle was very ill with the plague and was dying, and that he was on his way to the church of Tlatelolco to call for a priest to administer the last rites. He told Her that he had every good intention of coming back some other time for Her sign that he would take to the Bishop.

With heartfelt understanding, the Lady answered him, **"There is nothing to fear. Do not worry about your uncle's illness, or any other illness or vicissitude. Am I not your loving mother? Am I not life and health? Do you need anything else? Do not be anxious. Your uncle will not die from this illness. Believe that he is already cured."**

As it was learned later, at that precise moment his uncle was healed.

Juan Diego was relieved, and his heart was appeased by Her miraculous and marvelous words. In buoyant spirits, he offered his services. "My Lady, what is the sign that I shall take to the Bishop?"

She instructed him to climb to the top of the little hill, where he had first seen Her. **"There you will find a variety of flowers. Cut them, gather them up, put them together in your ayate and bring them here, to my presence."** Juan Diego was wondering what flowers would be there, because it was wintertime. The land was covered with frost, and was barren of vegetation. Besides, flowers never grew on that rocky hill. Only the prickly pear, mesquite, and other woody thorns struggled to sprout in those rugged and steep crags. Keeping those thoughts in his heart, he obeyed, and did exactly as the Lady had ordered him to do. When he reached the hilltop where he had first seen Her, he found a glorious garden with a diversity of species of beautiful flowers in full bloom. Exquisite Castillian red roses were glistening with pearls of dew. Their delightful fragrance permeated the cool air. In awe, he picked as many as he could hold in his tilma. He brought them down to the Lady, who was waiting for him by a spider lily tree. The Indians call this tree, 'ayuno' (fasting), because it bears no fruit, only umbels of white flowers in the spring. Our Lady took the roses with Her precious hands, and carefully arranged them on the piece of burlap that hung from Juan Diego's neck. She said to him, **"This is the sign that you will take to the Bishop, so that he may believe. Tell him everything - how I ordered you to climb to the top of this little hill to cut the flowers, and all that you have marveled at and admired. Show the flowers to no one but him. This is the proof, the evidence that will convince the Bishop of my wish that a temple be built here in my honor. I have great confidence and trust in you. You are my messenger and my ambassador."**

"Thank you, my Lady and my Child for the honor of serving you. I will carry out your bidding, immediately." Joyous and confident that this time his mission would succeed, Juan Diego set out to call on the Bishop. Holding his precious bundle close to his heart, he took the usual causeway that lead directly to Tenochtitlan. Juan Diego felt exhilarated, not so much by the nippy wind, but by his sacred mission at hand. Walking at a fast pace, he made his way to the city, peeking now and then at the beautiful flowers and enjoying the delightful fragrance of the roses.

When he arrived at the Bishop's home, the porter and other servants met him at the gate. Juan Diego begged them to tell their master that it was imperative that he see him. But the servants ignored him, because they had heard from their companions that he was a charlatan and a liar. Juan Diego refused to leave. Standing with his head bowed, he waited patiently. He was determined to wait for as long as necessary, just in case he was called. The servants checked now and then to see if he was still waiting at the gate. They became curious when they noticed that the Mazeuhalli was carrying 'something' in his tilma. So they came over to him, and attempted to pull his ayate. At first, Juan Diego resisted, but then he became afraid that they would continue harassing him and tear his cape. When he saw that it was impossible to conceal the contents of his bundle, he allowed the prying, pesky, peons to pull a corner of his tilma, and they saw the roses. They attempted to touch the roses three times, but to their amazement, their hands could only touch something that seemed to be a painting on the piece of burlap. The bewildered servants ran to tell the Bishop of their bizarre experience with the flowers that the little Indian was carrying in his ayate. "He is the same one who has come before to see you, your Excellency. He is back again, and has been waiting for a long time, he says that it is very important that you see him."

When he heard this, the Bishop knew that Juan Diego had brought the sign. Burning with curiosity, he immediately called him into his office. The servants and other people followed Juan Diego inside. When Juan Diego saw the Bishop, he bowed and narrated exactly the Lady's message to him. "Your Eminence, the Lady, the little Heavenly Maiden, has sent you proof so that you may believe me. She sends you beautiful, fragrant Castillian roses, which She commanded me to cut at the rocky crag of Tepeyac. This morning, the top of the hill looked like Paradise. Where only thorny plants like the mesquite and the prickly pear manage to survive, there was a gorgeous garden full of exquisite, fragrant, fresh flowers, shimmering with dewdrops like lustrous pearls. She said, **'Tell the Bishop that it is I, the Mother of God, who send you again to see him and to ask that he build my sacred house here, in this hillock of Tepeyac.'** Your Excellency, so that you may believe that I am telling you the truth, here is the Lady's sign." As Juan Diego unfolded his tilma, the roses and the other flowers spilled to the floor. The Bishop was astonished and exalted by what he saw on Juan Diego's tilma, which was still tied around his neck. There, imprinted in glorious colors on the piece of sacking cloth was the most beautiful vision afforded to human eyes: the Image of the most Holy Virgin Mary, Our Lady of Guadalupe, exactly as She had appeared to Juan Diego at Tepeyac. The Bishop threw himself on his knees, his eyes glistening with tears, tears as bright as the dew on the mystical roses before him. Fray Zumarraga, weeping and with great sadness, begged Our Lady's forgiveness for not having believed Her sacred words and obeyed Her supreme will. He got up, untied the tilma from Juan Diego's neck and took it to his chapel. Afterwards, the Bishop de Zumarraga invited Juan Diego to be his houseguest.

The next day Juan Diego took the Bishop to the site where the Mother of God had appeared to him, reminiscing over all the wonderful things that he had witnessed, marveled at and admired. Then, Juan Diego asked to be excused to go home and see his uncle, who had been very ill when he had left for the church in Tlatelolco to fetch a priest. He told the Bishop, "Yesterday, at dawn, as I was on my way to the city, Our Heavenly Mother met me by the little hill and told me not to worry or be anxious, because my uncle was not going to die from the plague, and that he was already cured."

The Bishop did not let him go alone. He sent Juan Diego home accompanied by dignitaries and members of his household staff. When they arrived at the home of Juan Bernardino, they found him well and happy. He wanted to know why the Spaniards honored his nephew in such a grand manner. Juan Diego then related to his uncle the events of the previous day, when he met the Mother of God on his way to fetch a priest. Juan Bernardino told his nephew that he had also seen the Lady at that hour, exactly as She had appeared to him. After healing Juan Bernardino, Our Lady had urged him, "Go to Mexico and see the Bishop. Tell him everything that you have seen, and the marvelous manner in which I have healed you. Also, tell him that my precious and beloved Image should be named: EVER VIRGIN HOLY MARY OF GUADALUPE."

Our Lady's request was immediately honored. Bishop Juan de Zumarraga and the people of Mexico built a temple at the bottom of the little hill, where a humble Mazeuhalli named Juan Diego had had the honor and the privilege of seeing and speaking with the Mother of God.

Throughout the centuries Her blessed and beloved Image has been cherished and preserved, exactly as it miraculously appeared on Juan Diego's tilma on December 12, 1531.

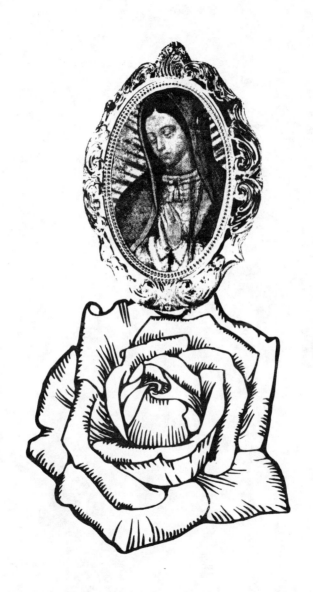

XVII CENTURY ENGRAVING OF JUAN DIEGO
COURTESY OF THE JOHN CARTER BROWN LIBRARY AT BROWN UNIVERSIT

15

WHO WAS THIS BLESSED JUAN DIEGO?

History tells us that Juan Diego was born in 1474 in Cuauhtitlan, a town which had been established in 1168 by the people of Nahua, and conquered by the Aztec lord Axayactl in 1467. Cuauhtitlan was fourteen miles north of Tenochtitlan, which is now known as Mexico City.

Juan Diego's native name was Cuauhtlatoatzin, meaning in Nahuatl, 'Talking Eagle.' Very little is known about his personal life, except that in 1516 at age 42, he married a Nahuan woman, whose name was Malintzin. They had no children, but their marriage was a happy one. He also had an uncle, whom Our Lady healed during the Fourth Apparition to Juan Diego. In 1525 Cuauhtlatoatzin and his wife and uncle were baptized and converted to Catholicism. Their Baptist was Fray Toribio de Benavente, whom the Indians called "Motolina" (the poor one), for his compassionate and benevolent nature. The new Christians were given the names of Juan Diego, Maria Lucia, and Juan Bernardino, respectively.

Long before his conversion and the apparitions, Juan Diego was a religious man with deep devotion to the Virgin Mary. Every Saturday, he walked the fourteen miles from Cuauhtitlan to the church in Tenochtitlan to hear mass in Her honor. He was a loner, prone to long periods of silence. A mystical man, who fasted frequently, and faithfully did penance. Prayer and meditation were his favorite pastime.

The Nican Mopohua tells us that Juan Diego was a Mazeuhalli, a member of the lowest class in the Aztec Empire. Although he was considered a poor native by the Spaniards, and thought of himself as a 'nobody' as he told Our Lady, he was somewhat prosperous and fairly educated. He had a mat-making business, and owned a house on a parcel of land in Cuauhtitlan. After his wife died in 1529, in grief he moved to Tolpetlac, where he built another house near that of his beloved uncle, Juan Bernardino.

After the apparitions, Juan Diego gave his houses and properties to Juan Bernardino. Bishop Juan de Zumarraga built Juan Diego a small house by the newly erected temple of Our Lady of Guadalupe, where Juan Diego spent the last seventeen years of his life. He had the honor and the pleasure of looking after his Lady's 'casita' himself. He kept repeating the marvelous story of his encounter with the Mother of God to the many daily visitors in Tepeyac.

On May 30, 1548, at the age of 74, Our Lady took him to Heaven.

Bishop de Zumarraga died four days after Juan Diego, on June 3, 1548.

In his 1675 <u>Felicidad de Mexico</u>, page 19, Luis Bezerra Tanco states that Maria Lucia died in 1534, two years after the apparitions. However, in his 1649 <u>Huei Tlamahuicoltica</u>, page 79, #306 & #307, Luis Lasso de la Vega tells us that Maria Lucia died in 1529, and that Juan Diego was a widower when the Mother of God appeared to him in 1531.

In the same publication, page 81, #313, Luis Lasso de la Vega also states that when Juan Diego's uncle Juan Bernardino, became ill with the plague again, he had a dream and saw the Lady. She told him that it was time for him to leave this world, that he should not fear death, and that She would be with him at the time of his passing. He died on May 25, 1544, at the age of 84. He is buried beside Juan Diego in the 'Capilla del Cerrito' in Tepeyac.

THE GUADALUPAN TESTIMONIES OF 1666

In addition to the 1556 inquest of the miracle of Guadalupe, a second inquiry was held in 1666 in which the elderly Aztecs of Cuauthtitlan, (Don Gabriel Juarez, Don Andres Juan, Doña Juana de la Concepcion, Don Pablo Juarez, Don Martin de San Luis, Don Juan Juarez, and Doña Catarina Monica) and a group of Spaniards testified to having learned from their families and friends about the miraculous apparitions of Our Lady of Guadalupe. Their testimonies were heard from January 7th through the 22[d] in the presence of Antonio Sebastian de Toledo Molina y Salazar (the Marquis de Mancera), the Ecclesiastical Chapter, and other dignitaries of Mexico. The assemblage unanimously voted to have the Image examined by the country's most acclaimed art experts: Nicolas de Angulo, Sebastian Lopez de Avalos, Br. Tomas Conrado, Nicolas de Fuen Labrada, Lic. Juan Salguero, Juan Sanchez, and Alonso de Zarate. They would be allowed to touch the Sacred Image on Juan Diego's tilma.

On March 20, 1666, accompanied by Dr. Francisco de Siles, Fr. Francisco de Florencia, and Lic. Luis Becerra Tanco, the artists meticulously examined the miraculous work of art. To their amazement, they discovered many mysteries: at first sight, they felt that it would be impossible to make with human hands such fine art on such a rough, stiff, and unprepared piece of burlap. They were fascinated by the mixture of media on the painting. With wonder, they admired the vivid colors and the gold of the border and the stars on Our Lady's mantel. They found large blotches of various colors on the back of the tilma. A large one in the center had the most exquisite shades of green, which did not correspond to the color scheme on the front of the Image. While the reverse side of the painting felt rough and stiff, as a cactus cloth should, the obverse side felt soft and smooth. They knew that their burning questions would remain unanswered. The artists took an oath, attesting that the 'canvas' lacked preparation or sizing. They unanimously agreed that only God knew the secret of how this magnificent likeness of Our Lady could have been achieved on an unprepared piece of maguey cloth and kept in perfect condition for so many years.

Shortly after the painters inspected the Image, the University Professors and the Examining Board of Royal Physicians (Dr. Lucas de Cardenas Soto, Dr. Geronimo Ortiz, and Dr. Juan de Melgarejo) also examined the tilma. They were accompanied again by Dr. Don Francisco de Siles, Lic. Luis Becerra Tanco, and Fr. Francisco de Florencia. Like the artists, they made startling discoveries and asked themselves many questions. They were mystified by three phenomena in particular. First, how was it possible that the painting on the porous and coarse maguey cactus 'canvas' remained unblemished, totally intact after being exposed to a briny and sultry environment for 135 years? The chapel where the Sacred Painting was kept was surrounded by craggy hills containing corrosive minerals. Also, the polluted lake Texcoco and a swampy river were nearby. When the waters of the lake receded, they left a border of saltpeter dust. During dry weather the winds blew this powdery sodium nitrate onto the rocks, grinding them into sand. This maleficent and corrosive wind also turned silver objects black. Why, then, had not this fragile cactus cloth decayed? (Even today, four and a half centuries after the miracle, the ayate and the colors of Her painting remain undamaged and vivid).

Ignacio Carrillo y Perez tells us in his 1797 book, Pensil Americano, that in addition to the briny atmosphere that destroyed paintings and buildings, rusted iron, and even damaged silver, that the Image was unshielded until 1647, 116 years after the miracle, due to the shortage of glass at that time. The Image was exposed to the vapor and soot of many candles, and to the flames of more than sixty lamps that were kept burning in the church. Also, the Sacred Image has endured the friction of millions of holy cards, medals and rosaries. Had the Icon been made of iron, it would have already corroded and been destroyed.

Second, after tenderly and carefully examining the tilma, Dr. Siles and his colleagues, like the artists, found on the back center of the 'canvas' a large, oval stain in the most beautiful shades of green. It had soaked into the porous fabric; however, it could not be detected from the front.

Third, having touched the back of the tilma, they too felt the stiffness and roughness of the cactus cloth, but the front of the tilma was mysteriously satin-smooth and soft. As requested by the Royal Board, the physicians wrote their reports after examining the tilma. When Dr. Juan de Melgarejo wrote his report on March 28, 1666, with regard to the third phenomenon he stated: "Who knows how this can be comprehended? My limited intelligence is not sufficient."

With reference to the colored stains found on the back of the tilma, in his book La Estrella del Norte de Mexico, Father Francisco de Florencia tells us of another time when, accompanied by Dr. Francisco de Siles and other colleagues, he examined the back of the Sacred Painting. Although the painting was translucent, while holding it to the light they observed that the shadow of the Image could not be seen from the back. All they could see were blotches of colors, like the squeezed juice of various flowers and their leaves, which could not be detected on the front of the painting. Although the colors were integrated, they were unmistakably discrete. They could distinguish the green of the leaves of white lilies, and the snowy white color of the flower, the purplish color of the day-lily, the blush shade of the rose, the vivid blue of violets, and the bright yellow of the broom plant. The men contemplated the confusion of colors, commenting as to which color belonged to which flower. Finally, they concluded that it appeared as though the Image had not been painted with an artist's brush, but stamped with a seal, the size of the Image. It seemed as though the flowers that Juan Diego had carried in his tilma were put through a torculo (small press), which extracted their juice and that of their leaves and stems. After having used the necessary amount of juice to create the painting, the remaining fluid had soaked through to the back of the tilma, leaving the large stain that they were admiring.

THE MYSTERIES OF THE TILMA

Throughout the centuries, all over the world, Our Lady has been making apparitions to Her chosen emissaries on earth. However, this is the first and only time in which She so graciously has left an actual likeness of Herself.

The mysteries of the tilma have been baffling artists, scientists, and scholars since the sixteenth century. One does not have to have the probing mind of a scientist or to hold a master's degree in fine art to wonder how such an exquisite portrait could possibly have been achieved on a crude cactus canvas. It is not surprising that even the church dignitaries' curiosity was sufficiently aroused that they retained an expert to examine the Icon on the tilma. The highly acclaimed seventeenth century painter, Miguel Cabrera, was commissioned in 1751 by the Most Reverend Jose Manuel Rubio y Salinas, Archbishop of Mexico, to examine the miraculous Image on the tilma with a group of highly acclaimed painters: Jose de Ibarra, Manuel de Osorio, Juan Patricio Morlete Ruiz, Francisco Antonio Vallejo, Jose de Alcibar, and Jose Ventura Arnaes. Mr. Cabrera not only had the church's permission to investigate the artistic techniques employed to create this mysterious work of art, but he was allowed to touch the Image with his own hands. In his 1756 publication <u>Maravilla Americana</u>, Mr. Cabrera tells us that on April 30, 1751, assisted by this group of renowned painters of his time, he meticulously examined the Sacred Image. He wrote a well-detailed report of the many startling discoveries that he and his team made during their analyses of the tilma. Above all, they were astonished to find that such a masterpiece could have been created on a rough and loosely woven maguey 'canvas.' They found that this 'canvas' was without primer, totally unprepared for laying the various mixtures of media. They agreed that four different media had been used to create the marvelous masterpiece. First, Mr. Cabrera points out that Our Lady's head and hands were done in oil, for which a properly prepared canvas is imperative.

Second, the Virgin's tunic, the angel, and the clouds were executed in tempera, a pigment base mixed with water-soluble, glutinous materials made from glue, wax, clay or egg yolk. Third, watercolor was used for Her mantel: watercolor is usually applied on a white, thin-faced canvas moistened on the back. Finally, the background surrounding the golden rays was painted with a combination of two media: a mixture of fresco and distemper, consisting of a compounded pigment dissolved in water, mixed with a casein binder, and applied to the canvas with a palette knife. This technique is only used for painting on a firm and moist plaster surface, such as a wall. Mr. Cabrera affirms that these four media are so diverse that they would require separate canvases, each prepared differently. He also states that he was unsuccessful when he tried to duplicate the painting using the same coarse material and the four media used on the tilma. The results were crude and inharmonious, lacking the breathtaking grace and beauty of the original.

When describing the gold that embellishes the enchanting portrait, this skilled and respected artist said that the gold 'paint' found on this fascinating painting is truly extraordinary. He claims that it is the most exquisite golden color that he has ever seen. Mr. Cabrera states that when he first saw this lustrous, metallic, golden tone, it appeared to be a powdery decoration. He was hesitant to touch it, or even to breathe on it for fear that it might disperse. Having been given the church's permission to handle the tilma, he did so with the reverence demanded by the Sacred Image. During his palpation of the gold on the tilma, he considered the manner in which this golden medium was applied to the cactus cloth. It appeared as though the gold had either been applied to the threads before they were woven, or stamped directly onto the fibers of the sacking cloth. The areas that were 'painted' with this mysterious golden tone were closely and tightly interwoven. The concavity of the fabric could only be detected by touch.

Another startling discovery was the strange golden design of the flowers on Her tunic. This exquisite work was of rare skill: the shapes of the flowers were outlined with a clean, three-dimensional vein of gold, as thin as a strand of hair. This marvel can only be perceived at a short distance. This famous artist concurred with his colleagues that this technique of painting was unheard of, that they had never seen it done before. The marvelous three-dimensional, golden 'embroidery' on Her tunic has been greatly admired over the centuries by the fortunate people who have been close to Her portrait. Mr. Cabrera admits that it was impossible for him to surmise the technique used to apply this three-dimensional golden pigment. Finally, he adds that he could only compare this mystical golden hue to the dusty gold found on the wings of colorful and beautiful butterflies.

Reverently detailing Our Lady's Image, Mr. Cabrera made the following conjectures. It was not by chance that Our Lady placed Her beloved Image at a specific angle on the 'canvas.' It was Her plan to avoid having the seam of the tilma mar Her lovely face. Thus, She tilted Her beautiful face to the right, barely missing the hand-stitching which holds the two pieces of maguey fabric together. Her face is exquisitely depicted: the profiles of Her eyes, nose and mouth are done so finely that they captivate the hearts of those who have seen the actual masterpiece. Her black hair is simply styled in the fashion worn by the noble women of that time. Our Lady's eyes are downcast; Her gaze is gentle and compassionate, evoking inner peace, joy, and reverence.

Another mystery is that of the fragile maguey thread, which for centuries has been holding together the two heavy pieces of maguey sacking. To this day, the thread, like the paint on the marvelous portrait, remains in perfect condition. Time has not touched this marvelous work of art. Mr. Cabrera insists that the painting on the tilma is one of a kind, impossible to duplicate. "His work is perfect!" (Deut. 32:4). According to him it could not be presumed that our Lady's portrait was humanly made. The results of the artistic analyses made on the tilma have removed the clouds of doubt from the minds of the many skeptics who for so many years have subjected the miraculous piece of burlap to the scrutiny of their experiments.

In view of his findings, Mr. Cabrera believes that this painting cannot be anything but supernatural. He ends by solemnly affirming that, *"This case in point is so indisputably convincing that I believe this painting is a miracle!"* "Great are the works of the Lord." (Ps. 111:2).

Miguel Cabrera was born in Tlalixtac (now Oaxaca), Mexico, on February 27, 1695. He arrived in Mexico City in 1719 at the age of 24, and studied under Juan Correa. His early works were paintings of saints, which are in the Queretaro Museum; they are signed and dated 1741. Miguel Cabrera was the official painter of His Excellency, Most Rev. Jose Manuel Rubio y Salinas, Archbishop of Mexico. He specialized in portraiture, and painted many beautiful portraits of Our Lady of Guadalupe. In 1753 Mr. Cabrera founded the first academy of art in Mexico City. His most important works are at the National Museum in Chapultepec: the portrait of Sister Juana Ines de la Cruz, and the Viceroy Don Francisco de Guemes y Horcasitas. In the church of San Francisco of St. Luis Potosi, there is a collection of eight paintings: six about the life of St. Anthony, and two about the life of St. Clara. In the mid-seventeen hundreds he obtained his most important commissions. He painted a total of thirty canvases about the lives of St. Ignacio Loyola for the School of St. Ignacio, and of St. Dominic, for St. Dominic's Convent. His magnificent painting of the Last Supper is in the Sacristy of St. Jeronimo Aculco. He also painted various portraits of saints, which are in the Academy of San Carlos. His self-portrait is at the National Museum of Plastic Arts. He was the most famous, prolific painter of the viceroyalty period. His large number of paintings are scattered over many providences of Mexico. Mr. Cabrera's paintings have a Rubenesque touch. He died in Mexico City on May 16, 1768.

"The Miracle of Guadalupe" by Miguel Cabrera, XVII century Mexican Painter.
Courtesy of His Excellency Monsignor Norberto Rivera C., Archbishop of Mexico

Notice the stitching on the vertical seam on the left side of the tilma. Throughout the centuries this flimsy maguey cactus thread has held the two pieces of the heavy coarse ayate together.

◘ ◘ ◘

In their book, <u>Descubrimiento de un Busto Humano en los Ojos de la Virgen de Guadalupe</u>, Carlos Salinas and Manuel de la Mora documented reports from the following eminent ophthalmologists and surgeons: Dr. Enrique Graue, Dr. Eduardo Turati Alvarez, Dr. Javier J.Torroella, Dr. Rafael Torija Lavoignet, Dr. Amado Jorge Kuri, Dr. Ismael Ugalde Nieto, Dr. A. Jayme Palacios, Dr. Jose Roberto Ahued A., Dr. Guillermo Silva Rivera, and Dr. Ernestina Zavaleta, who after having examined Our Lady of Guadalupe's eyes on Juan Diego's tilma unanimously agreed to having found the Purkinje-Sanson reflections in Our Lady's eyes.

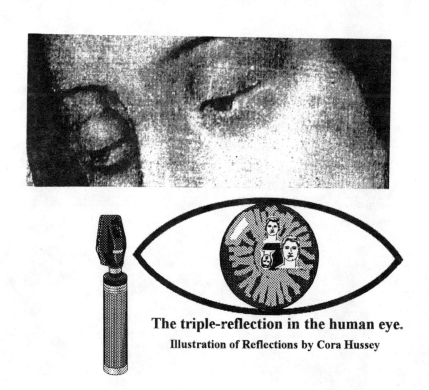

The triple-reflection in the human eye.
Illustration of Reflections by Cora Hussey

DR. ENRIQUE GRAUE

◘ ◘

In 1974 and 1975 Dr. Enrique Graue examined Our Lady's eyes using a high-power ophthalmoscope, allowing him to appreciate the Purkinje-Sanson images. His visual sensation was that of depth. Dr. Graue saw the bust of a man reflected in the corneas of Our Lady's eyes. He comments on having had the feeling of looking into a live eye, which made him thinks of something supernatural.

DR. EDUARDO TURATI ALVAREZ

◘ ◘

According to Dr. Eduardo Turati Alvarez' statement of December 10, 1975, during his examination he also found the images reflected in Our Lady's eyes in the positions corresponding to the Purkinje-Sanson reflections. Dr. Alvarez states that when focusing his ophthalmoscope on the Virgin's right eye he had the sensation of depth and he could appreciate the curvature on the surface of the cornea. He points out that he did not see this phenomenon on any of the other paintings that he was asked to examine.

DR. JAVIER J. TORROELLA

◘ ◘

In his report of February 21, 1976, Dr. Javier J. Torroella states that he also found the Purkinje-Sanson images in both of Our Lady's eyes. While examining the Virgin's eyes with a loupe he discovered the image of a bearded man in both Her eyes. The images are in the correct place with respect to the position of Our Lady's head: internal in the right eye and external in the left.

The reflection of the image in the left eye is not as clear as the one in the right eye. This is as it should be, since the Virgin's right eye is closer to the person at whom she is looking.

Dr. Torroella explains the Purkinje-Sanson catoptric triple-image reflections in this manner: If we put a light in front of an eye, its reflection is easily seen in the cornea. An image reflects from three places in the eye: on the anterior surface of the cornea, on the anterior surface of the crystalline lens, and on its posterior. The characteristics of these images are as follows: The image of the anterior surface of the cornea is very brilliant and erect. The second image on the anterior surface of the crystalline lens is also erect, but less brilliant, and the third is inverted and less luminous. In order to observe these last two images, it is necessary to dilate the pupil, since these images are found behind the iris.

The reflections of the images in Our Lady of Guadalupe's eyes which Dr. Torroella studied are found in the cornea. The cornea is neither flat nor spherical. Thus, it produces a distortion of the image in accordance with the place from which it is reflected. If an image is reflected in the temporal region of the right eye, it will reflect from the nasal area of the left eye. In this case according to Dr. Torroella, the images are perfectly, relatively located. The distortion of the figure is also in accordance with the curvature of the cornea.

DR. RAFAEL TORIJA LAVOIGNET
◘ ◘

Dr. Rafael Torija Lavoignet states that he examined Our Lady of Guadalupe's eyes on five occasions. The first was at the beginning of July 1956, the second was on July 23rd of the same year, the third and fourth on February 16th and 20th, 1957, and the last on May 26th, 1958. The following are highlights of his findings, which he certifies. In the cornea of Our Lady's right eye, clearly visible, he found the image of a human bust. Besides the human bust, Dr. Lavoignet observed two more luminous reflections. The three reflections correspond to the three images of the Purkinje-Sanson reflections. The image on Our Lady's eye appears distorted. This distortion is a normal correlative to the curvature of the cornea. The image's reflection is also evident on the surface of the iris.

Dr. Lavoignet explains that when one directs the light of one's ophthalmoscope to the pupil of a human eye, a brilliant reflection is seen in the external curvature of the iris. When one changes the ophthalmoscope lens, the reflection is perceived in the depth of the eye. Dr. Lavoignet aimed the ophthalmoscope's light at the pupil of the Virgin's eye and a luminous reflection appeared at every angle. The light is brilliant and can be seen at every distance in Her eye. He says that this phenomenon can be perceived at a glance! Dr. Lavoignet affirms that it should have been impossible to obtain this reflection from a flat and opaque surface such as the one of the painting.

He further asserts that the luminous reflection of the human bust in Our Lady's cornea is not an optical illusion caused by the texture of the ayate.

Dr. Lavoignet adds that he has examined various people's eyes on oil paintings and photographs with his ophthalmoscope, and none showed any reflections like the ones he saw in Our Lady's portrait. He concludes by saying that the Image of Our Lady of Guadalupe gives the impression of vitality!

DR. AMADO JORGE KURI

◘ ◘

In his report of August 19, 1975, Dr. Kuri states that when he examined the Image on Juan Diego's ayate, he observed that Our Lady's eyes were gazing at an object in front of Her, downward and toward the right.

With his loupe he examined the corneas and irises, which are perfectly painted with a brilliance that gives the impression of a pair of live eyes. During his examination he had the sensation of seeing through the crystalline lenses. The iris in the Virgin's right eye is not totally rounded; in the extreme left, toward the lacrimal punctum, the contour breaks with the presence of an orange, human image that is somewhat distorted. The head, neck, upper thorax and shoulder with an arm extended can be discerned. A portion of the arm is situated in the circular area of the iris. There are luminous spots on both the posterior and anterior of the crystalline lens. The posterior one is smaller and less brilliant.

Dr. Kuri closes by saying that the three luminous reflections of the right eye, more than the left, keep the proportional sizes and spacing so perfect and so clear that they are consistent with the characteristic of the Purkinje-Sanson reflections.

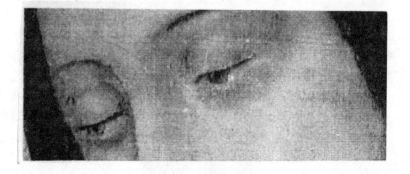

DR. ISMAEL UGALDE NIETO

◘ ◘

Dr. Nieto has verified Dr. Torroella's findings. He confirms that there is a human image in the corneas of Our Lady of Guadalupe's eyes.

DR. A. JAYME PALACIOS

◘ ◘

Dr. Palacios states that he observed in the eyes of Our Lady of Guadalupe, whose Sacred Image is on the original ayate kept in the major altar of the Basilica of Guadalupe, the bust of a man symmetrically placed and corresponding to the corneal reflections, according to the optical laws.

DR. JOSE ROBERTO AHUEDA

◘ ◘

Dr. Ahueda confirms Dr. Kuri's findings. He states that the ocular exploratory examination of Our Lady's eyes was like that of a live person. The three luminous reflections of the right eye, more than the left, have the proportional sizes and spacing of the Purkinje-Sanson reflections.

DR. GUILLERMO SILVA RIVERA

◘ ◘

Dr. Rivera also agrees with the reports of Dr. Torija Lavoignet and Dr. Torroella. He attests to having been able to see clearly (without any examining instrument), the image of a human bust situated in the corneas of Our Lady of Guadalupe's eyes. The image is normally distorted in accordance with the curvature of the cornea. Its brilliant reflections correspond to the Purkinje-Sanson's description of the reflection of images in the eye.

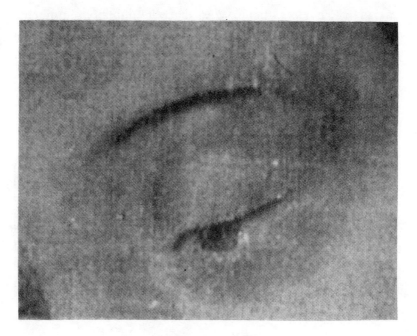

Our Lady's Left Eye

DR. ERNESTINA ZAVALETA

◘ ◘

Dr. Zavaleta also agrees with Dr. Torija Lavoignet's and Dr. Torroella's findings. She attests to having observed a human bust in the corneas of Our Lady of Guadalupe's eyes, whose Image is on the ayate kept in the major altar of the Basilica of Guadalupe. Dr. Zavaleta states that the image of the human bust is clearly visible without the need of any optical instruments, and is distorted according to the curvature of the cornea.

Dr. Zavaleta emphasizes that the luminous reflections correspond precisely to the Purkinje-Sanson reflections.

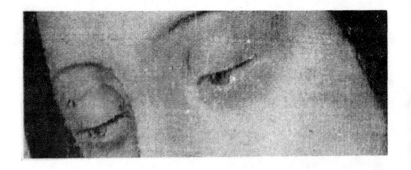

DR. JOHANNES EVANGELISTA VON PURKYNE

■ ◘ ■

Johannes Evangelista von Purkyne was born on December 17, 1787 in Libochovice, Bohemia (now Czechoslovakia). Later on he shortened and changed his name to Jan Evangelista Purkinje, so as to have it pronounced correctly. Dr. Jan Evangelista Purkinje studied physiology, histology, and embryology. However, his main interest was physiology. In 1819 he received his M.D.degree from the Charles University in Prague. Dr. Purkinje was an anatomy and pathology assistant professor at the University of Prague until 1823. That year King Frederick III of Prussia appointed him a professor of physiology and pathology in Breslau (Wroclaw), a city in southwest Poland, on the Oder River. He was chairman of the Department of Physiology at the University of Breslau in 1823, when he discovered the catoptric images from the crystalline lens, and recommended their use for eye examinations.

In 1827 he married and had two sons. His wife died in 1835, and he never remarried. In 1849 he returned to Prague, where he remained a professor of physiology until his death on July 28, 1869.

Dr. LOUIS-JOSEPH SANSON

◘ ◘ ◘

In his 1986 multi volume publication <u>The History of Ophthalmology</u>, Julius Hirsberg tells us that Dr. Louis-Joseph Sanson, Sr. was born on January 24, 1790 in Nogent-sur-Seine, France.

In 1837 independently of Dr. Purkinje, he discovered the catoptric triple-image reflections in the eye. He also used them for diagnosing ocular diseases. Dr. Sanson published many books on general surgery. He contributed articles on amaurosis, cataract, glaucoma and ophthalmia to the <u>Dictionnaire de Medecine et Chrirugie Pratiques</u>.

He died young on August 2, 1841.

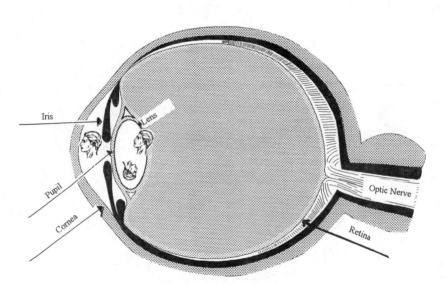

THE PURKINJE-SANSON REFLECTIONS
Illustration of Reflections by Cora Hussey

An Enlargement of Our Lady's Eyes

"A COMPASSIONATE GAZE THAT FILLS OUR HEARTS WITH FAITH, HOPE AND LOVE." *C.H.*

"YOUR EYES ARE LIKE DOVES" (S. of S. 4:1).

My intention in writing this brief report on Our Lady's eyes as they appear on the tilma is merely to give the reader a glimpse of Dr. Jose Aste Tonsmann's amazing discoveries in the Virgin's eyes, as reported in his book: Los Ojos de la Virgen de Guadalupe. Therefore, I will not address his studies in depth; only some of the results of his findings in Our Lady's mysterious eyes will be highlighted. Besides Dr. Tonsmann's computer studies, there is a tremendous amount of data from other studies: intensive inspections by renowned artists, ophthalmological examinations, and infrared photography. Many scientists who have examined the eyes in the painting have verified that the images reflected in both Her eyes are in the precise location they would be in the live human eye. However, my booklet is not intended as a scientific study, but as an introduction to the miraculous apparitions at Tepeyac.

If we ever had any doubt about Our Lady's miraculous Image on the tilma, all we would need to do is to look into Her eyes, and every molecule of our misgivings would evaporate. Truly, those fascinating and inspiring eyes look alive and gleaming. Her tranquil and compassionate gaze fills our hearts with faith, hope and love.

The purpose of Dr. Tonsmann's study was to investigate the bust of an image that had been discovered in the right eye of Our Lady by a painter named Carlos Salinas in 1951. Mr. Salinas is the co-author of Descubrimiento de un Busto Humano en los Ojos de la Virgen de Guadalupe.

Dr. Tonsmann tells the reader that, "since in a live person images reflect only in the iris," he focused his study on analyzing the "two irises" in the Virgin's eyes. Dr. Tonsmann, who is an environmental systems engineer, used a computer process called digitalization to analyze clear photographs of the actual painting, in black and white and in color. His photo enlargements ranged from thirty times to two thousand times the size of the original. He used many types of filters during his magnification process of the microscopic image-reflections in the Virgin's eyes, making startling discoveries.

He reminds us that the "irises" on the painting measure only approximately seven to eight millimeters. The material on which the Image is imprinted is coarse and totally unsuitable for minute detailing.

First, Dr. Tonsmann discovered the image of a crossed-legged, almost naked Mazeuhalli sitting on the floor, in the extreme right of the Virgin's left "iris." The image's extended left foot clearly shows that he is wearing sandals: even the fastening strap is visible. His forehead appears to be shaved, as was the custom of the Aztecs, and his long hair is tied in a ponytail. He is also wearing earrings; the loop on his right ear is prominently visible. Only his face is noticeable in Our Lady's right eye. However, when an enlargement of his eye was made, it revealed the figure of a man with a large, aquiline nose, half opened eyes, and high cheek bones. It is assumed that it was the person at whom he was intently looking.

Dr. Tonsmann found another figure in Our Lady's left eye: an old, bearded Spaniard with a shiny, receding forehead, wearing a tonsure, like those worn by the friars of that period. He is looking down. He has a straight nose and a prominent chin; a tear appears to be spilling onto his cheek. This face amazingly resembles portraits of Bishop de Zumarraga.

Immediately to the left of the old man's face appears another figure: that of a very young man, perhaps the Bishop's translator, Juan Gonzalez. Bishop de Zumarraga did not speak Nahuatl, nor did Juan Diego speak Spanish.

Continuing with his search, Dr. Tonsmann found still another image that could be Juan Diego's. This figure has the face of a middle-aged man with high cheekbones, a large, aquiline nose, a goatee, and a meager mustache. He is wearing a hat shaped like a funnel, called a "cucurucho" (paper cone or coronet). The tilma is hanging from his neck, and his right arm is extended underneath it as he shows it to his audience.

These images, which are possibly those of Juan Diego, Fray Juan de Zumarraga and Juan Gonzalez, appear smaller and not as clearly in Our Lady's right eye.

In the extreme left of Our Lady's "iris," another bearded Spaniard is seen looking at the tilma. This is the bust that was discovered by the painter and author, Carlos Salinas. The image of this person is clearer in the right eye. This person could be a priest, who was present at the moment of the apparition. An interesting detail is that he is engrossed in thought, touching his beard with his right hand, his thumb hidden under his beard. His arm and shoulder can also be detected. The attitude of this image is one of the extreme interest and concentration, looking toward the area where the tilma is being unfolded.

In the center of the left eye, Dr. Tonsmann found an image of a group of Aztecs. The most obvious one because of her size and position is a young woman with delicate features. Her hair is coiffed like a rounded cap and secured with a "peineta" (a Spanish comb). She seems to be minding some children around her; most interesting of all is that she appears to be carrying a baby on her back held in a "rebozo" (shawl), as was the custom of Aztec women. Next to the woman is a man wearing a fancy hat, who appears to be in conversation with her. According to Dr. Tonsmann, this group is of major importance, because it is the tiniest of all the other characters visible in the left eye. In the right eye, the same images of this group of Aztecs are also seen, with the addition of more people: two other men are standing behind the woman with the baby on her back, and another woman and children are also present.

Dr. Tonsmann suggests that this tiny group visible in the eyes of the Virgin was intended as a message for us today. This is interesting, consisting that it was 450 years before the development of the necessary technology to allow us to discover it. After analyzing all the images in Our Lady's eyes, Dr. Tonsmann tells us that these images appear to be participants in two scenes:

The appearance of the Holy Virgin of Guadalupe on Juan Diego's tilma, and the congregating group of familiar Aztecs.

In the scene in which Our Lady's likeness is imprinted on the ayate, the tiny images are seen to be attentively contemplating the tilma that the one presumed to be Juan Diego has unfolded. Another detail of great importance is that of the sitting, almost naked Mazeuhalli on the extreme right of the left eye. He is engrossed in observing Juan Diego. His gesture of contemplation is one of pride, seeing another Mazeuhalli marvelously delighting so many Spaniards.

According to Dr. Tonsmann's theory, when the Bishop de Zumarraga received Juan Diego in his office, the Virgin was already present, invisible to them, viewing the entire scene. Therefore, the images that were in the room, including Juan Diego's, were reflected in her eyes. At the instant when Juan Diego unfolded his tilma and the flowers rolled to the floor, the Image of the Virgin appeared on the tilma. Her eyes have the reflections of what She saw at that moment: the group of people observing the event of Her apparition on the tilma.

Dr. Tonsmann attests to the following: **All the images found present on both eyes, in clearly different dimensions, angles and precision, are just as they would be reflected in the eyes of a live person, keeping relatively the same positions.**[1] **Even with the most advanced technology in the world, it would be impossible to "paint" images of those dimensions with the precision of so much detail, above all, in such coarse material like the one of the tilma that is in Tepeyac.**[2] "We can do nothing against the truth, only for it." (2 Cor. 13:8).

---

[1] Dr. Jose Aste Tonsmann, <u>Los Ojos de la Virgen de Guadalupe</u>, conslusion #1, p. 135.

[2] ibid, conclusion #5, p. 136.

I am neither a scientist nor an expert painter. Therefore, I am not qualified to evaluate the evidence presented by the eminent group of professionals who have examined Juan Diego's Tilma. I am simply an individual of average intelligence, with a profound and unwavering belief that the Mother of God indeed appeared to Juan Diego at Tepeyac. "How long will they not believe in me?" (Num. 14:11). When Our Lady was arranging the roses in Juan Diego's tilma, She told him, "This is the proof, the evidence that will convince the Bishop." I think that message was also intended for us all, because proof She left us! Our Lady left us tangible evidence, the beautiful likeness of Herself on an insignificant piece of burlap, so that we may believe that with God all things are possible.

I have written this so that your joy and mine may be complete!

A SALUTE AND TRIBUTE TO DR. JOSE ASTE TONSMANN!

<u>Los Ojos de la Virgen de Guadalupe</u> holds the reader spellbound. Dr. Tonsmann's astonishing discoveries and the magnified-photo results of his studies of Our Lady's eyes are overwhelming! It is thrilling to view the enlargements of the images found in Our Lady's eyes.

Dr. Tonsmann has broken through the barriers of time, transporting us to the sixteenth century. He invites the reader to the Bishop's palace in Tenochitlan, to witness the miraculous and memorable event that took place on that blessed morning of December 12, 1531. Dr. Tonsmann's theory is that the Virgin had to be present, immortalizing in her eyes forever the event of Her miracle! Dr. Tonsmann asserts that the images in Her eyes are definitely there. He affirms: **"Finally, we can prove the existence of the determined images."**[3]

I congratulate and applaud Dr. Tonsmann for his triumphant achievement. Indeed, he has given us another miracle! Dr. Tonsmann's electrifying discoveries in Our Lady of Guadalupe's eyes indicate that Our Lady Herself was present when She left Her Image on Juan Diego's tilma.

★

May the morning star
brighten your day.
May the evening star
illuminate your way.
May Our Lady always
bless the work of your hands.
Blessings,
Cora Hussey

---

[3] Dr. Jose Aste Tonsmann, <u>Los Ojos de la Virgen de Guadalupe</u>, p. 26, last paragraph.

43

FORGIVING FOR HEALTH
***

A Miraculous Cure by the Grace of Our Lady of Guadalupe

Text from DIVINE CONNECTIONS
A Trilogy of Spiritual Events

Love One Another!

The Love Rose
Oil on Canvas - 1991
Cora Hussey

"Forgive and you will be forgiven." (Matt. 6:14-15).

FORGIVING FOR HEALTH

On the evening of March 1, 1994, I was spending a quiet evening at home alone; it was my husband's tennis night. After a leisurely bath, I had supper in my bedroom, and watched TV. Because the arthritis on my right shoulder was bothering me, I took an over the counter tablet for pain. Twenty-seven minutes after having ingested the tablet, I became alarmingly ill with intense weakness all over my body, a racing heartbeat, and lightheadedness. Frantically, I tried to reach my doctor and my husband. I knew that there was something seriously wrong with me, so I went to unlock the electric gate and the front door so that the paramedics could find me. I was about to call 911, when my husband called to say that he was on his way. When Bern arrived, I could see that he was worried, "Honey, what's wrong?" he asked. I told him everything, and we tried to reach our doctor again. He told us that it could be a virus. Forty minutes later I felt a little better. However, the symptoms kept coming back, and as the days went by, my condition worsened. In addition to the original symptoms, digestive problems developed. I lost my appetite, and was losing weight rapidly: one pound per day. All that I could tolerate were a few sips of chicken broth, and water. My physical appearance was that of one seriously ill. I was as pale as candle-wax. I was so weak that I could hardly stand up. I was dying.

My physician saw me frequently, and he must have suspected something quite serious, because he ordered a myriad of tests, which all gave negative results. He was baffled, and his face was always solemn; he could not explain why I was so ill. We even discussed the possibility of a malignancy, but he said that the weakness, malaise, lack of appetite and drastic weight loss happens gradually when caused by a malignancy. Most distressful of all was the fact that I could not be hospitalized because there was no known cause for my illness.

There are no words to describe the ordeal and mental suffering that my husband and I went through during those thirty-five days that I was so mysteriously ill. During those darkest hours, Bern and I never stopped praying to Our Lady of Guadalupe for my recovery. I wanted so much to be healed. I didn't want to die yet; I had to finish writing my book, I wanted to see my daughter, Debbie, graduate from graduate school, I wanted to enjoy retirement with Bern in my dream cottage by the sea. There was so much that I had to live for, but "The cords of death surrounded me." (Ps. 18:4). When finally I knew that the end was near, a wonderful feeling of acceptance came over me. I simply relinquished all my human desires, and completely released myself to God's will. "Father, I put my life in your hands." (Luke 23:46). I felt calm, and enfolded by a comforting presence. I was at peace. God gave me the strength to get out of bed for short periods of time, to clean files and try to leave my husband with an easier task ahead. I have always been in charge of all the household and personal business, so I wanted to leave everything in order. I also tried to teach him my housekeeping routine, and how to cook his favorite foods. Bern was devastated to see me suffering so terribly - he too, lost weight. He cried often, and prayed constantly. We prayed persistently to Our Lady of Guadalupe for my complete recovery. As I continue to pray for my healing, the realization of the meaning of forgiveness came to light. How could I pray for my sins to be forgiven, if I did not first forgive others? "Forgive and you will be forgiven." (Matt. 6:14-15). Deep in my heart I knew that my body had been poisoned by something toxic in the tablet. But I also knew that I was carrying rancorous feelings and other spiritual impurities in my heart. It was clear what I had to do. Gravely ill as I was, I took a large garbage bag, and did the second and most important spring cleaning of my life. Many years ago, under different circumstances, I had done the same thing. However, I have the bad habit of cluttering my life, my home, and my mind with worthless nick-knacks and contemptuous thoughts. Since my last spiritual spring cleaning, I had accumulated a heavy load of bitterness, which was poisoning my soul. That day, I threw away every offensive letter that I had received and all my wrathful replies. I discarded a past of hate and anger. And, however I could, I wrote in bed, short notes to people against whom I held some resentment.

Then, one day as I was praying I thought of the words that this Lady of marvelous beauty had once said to the Mexican Indian, Juan Diego, on the Hill of Tepeyac, on December 9th and 12th, 1531 "...I am a Merciful Mother, to you and to all your fellow men on this earth who love me and trust me and invoke my help. Listen, my son, to what I tell you now: do not be troubled or disturbed by anything; do not fear illness or any other distressing occurrence, or pain. Am I not your Mother? Am I not life and health?" Weeping, I bowed my head and closed my eyes. How can I describe the beautiful vision that appeared in the inner recesses of my mind at that moment? Now I know why Jesus said that "The Kingdom of Heaven is within you." (Luke 17:21). Behold, Our Lady's glorious image, exactly as she had appeared to Juan Diego was glowing in my heart. The hillock where she stood serenely in majesty and splendor, glittered like precious jewels. Bright rays of light blazed like the sun from her garments, and all the brittle plants of the cliff dazzled with a rainbow of colors. I heard no voice, but I knew that my soul had made contact with the Divine. The seed to my cure was implanted in my thoughts almost instantly. "I will heal you." (2 Kgs.20:5). Her message that I should tell my doctor to order a lower GI test was deeply planted in me. I visualized my body being cleansed and rid of the toxic substance that had made me so terribly ill. Then, the vision left my mind just as quickly as it had come.

Immediately, Bern took me to our doctor and asked him for the test. He was skeptical, but he said it wouldn't hurt, adding, "But you'll be throwing your money away." Nevertheless, he agreed, and on Easter I began preparing for the test the next day. In the early morning of Monday, April 4th, the test was performed. A miracle happened! Our Lady of Guadalupe's revelation for me to have this test had saved my life! The barium had cleansed my intestinal lining of whatever poisonous residue was causing the horrible symptoms and slowly killing me. My healing had been instantaneous. I felt revived and vibrant, as though I had been born again. This must have been how Lazarus felt when he was brought back to life, and walked out of the tomb. Bern and I were ecstatic. From the laboratory we went directly to church to thank God and Our Lady of Guadalupe for my miraculous cure. When we were leaving the church I said to my husband, "Bernie, I'm hungry!" He hugged me and kissed me, and weeping with joy, we both made our way to my favorite cafeteria. I had a hearty breakfast of scrambled eggs, toast and coffee - my first meal in over a month. Afterwards, Bern took me to our doctor, who again could find nothing wrong with me. Only this time he was smiling, because he knew that I was healthy, and completely well again!

That day, Bern and I vowed to thank Our Lady of Guadalupe daily for the rest of our lives for having restored my health. And as a small token of my deep gratitude, I too, like Juan Diego, will always carry the message of Her merciful love to all her children.

Once my soul had been cleansed of ill feelings, my body was made clean again! By having forgiven others, I had truly forgiven myself. "I cried to you and you healed me." (PS. 30-2).

EPILOG

This near-death experience has changed my life. Now, I look at life through a new pair of binoculars; my perspective on life has changed. I do not take life for granted anymore. I am truly grateful for my good health, for the roof over my head, and for the food on my plate. Life is precious. Time is precious. Every day is a miracle.

My attitude also has changed; I am more humble. I discovered that humility is necessary for connecting the mind to divine power. The heart which humility inhabits cannot ferment rancor and hate. Rancor and hate are poisons catalysts that make the body sick, and the only antidote is Love.

Moreover, I realized that true happiness is not how much wealth one has, but how much health, because health is the most precious of all possessions. Health to me is real treasure.

The Mystical Rose of Tepeyac
Oil on Canvas - December 1994
Cora Hussey

This I Know!

Never underestimate the power of prayer. Prayer power is powerful. Moreover, believe in miracles. Therefore, start changing your thoughts about your illness. Now!

While doctors may say that you have a disease, know and believe with all your heart that the disease doesn't have you. God and Our Lady of Guadalupe can restore your health. Our Lady gave me back my life when I was dying of poisoning in 1994. Pray to Her; She is a merciful mother. Think of the promise Our Lady made to Juan Diego when She appeared to him on the hill of Tepeyac in 1531. She told him: "...do not fear illness or any other distressing occurrence, or pain. Am I not your Mother? Am I not life and health?" Therefore, begin right now by denying the disease! Every day, go to a quiet place, close your eyes and visualize yourself healthy and whole in every way. The Holy Spirit is doing the healing, not you or your doctor. Say aloud: "The Holy Spirit strengthens me, and I am healed." Allow the Holy Spirit of God to flow in your body and in your mind. Envision the healing coming forth. Deny the disease, and pretty soon it will have no power.

I have discovered that positive thoughts, and plenty of prayers are necessary to change our lives. Faith is the key. Believe with all your heart, and with all your soul, and as you believe it will be given to you. This I Know: Faith is the answer!

May the healing, shining light of Christ enfold you always.

Blessings,
Cora Hussey

Our Lady of Guadalupe **Patroness of the Americas**

"A Lady of Marvelous Beauty"

CHILD OF THE THIRD WORLD. COURTESY OF CORBIS-BETTMANN

Dear Reader,

I invite you to join me in prayer and ask Our Lady of Guadalupe to eradicate the famine in the world.

God Bless You!
Cora Hussey

"A Fervent Request"
By Cora Hussey

O dear Mother of Guadalupe, Our Queen, and Patroness of the world, remember your solemn promise to Juan Diego on the hill of Tepeyac: "I am a merciful Mother, and will hear your laments, remedy your misfortunes and ease your pain and suffering."

Therefore, we cast ourselves at your feet and join in prayer today to implore your help, to seek your intercession, and to ask that your compassionate gaze fall upon the starving children of the Third World, who so desperately need your aid.

May your infinite goodness heal and sustain them. Bestow on them your protection and nourish them with your love. Amen.

Note: Dear Readers, This is not intended as a fund-raising solicitation. But if you wish to share the works, you may send your donations to:

U.S. Committee for UNICEF, 333 East 38th St., New York, NY 10016

&

The Missionaries of Charity, 54A Acharya Jagadish Chandra Bose Road Calcutta, 700016, India

May Our Lady of Guadalupe bless you always.
With deep gratitude for your generosity,
Cora Hussey

Pray for World Peace

BIBLIOGRAPHY

Nican Mopohua by Guillermo Ortiz de Montellano. Published by Universidad Iberoamericana. Mexico, D.F. (1990). This is one of the best of the many Spanish translations that I have read of the original Nican Mopohua written in Nahuatl by the Aztec scholar Antonio Valeriano shortly before the death of Juan Diego in 1548.

Pensil Americano by Don Ignacio Carrillo y Perez. Published by D. Mariano J. De Zuniga y Ontiveros, Calle del Espiritu Santo, Mexico (1797).

Maravilla Americana by Miguel Cabrera. Imprenta del Real, y mas Antiguo Colegio de San Idelfonso. Mexico (1756).

Huei Tlamahuicoltica by B. Lic. Luis Lasso de la Vega, Vicar of Our Lady of Guadalupe Abbey in Mexico City, (in Nahuatl). Printed by Imprenta de Juan Ruiz in 1649. This work was a copy of the Nican Mopohua, translated into Spanish by Lic. Don Primo Feliciano Velazque. Printed in Mexico in 1926 by Carreno E Hijo, Editores.

Felicidad de Mexico by Luis Becerra Tanco. Published after his death in 1672, by Dr. D. Antonio Gama. Mexico (1675).

La Estrella del Norte de Mexico by Fr. Francisco de Florencia. Published by Imprenta de Antonio Velazquez, Barcelona, Spain (1741).

Tesoro Guadalupano by Fr. Fortino Hipolito Vera. Printers: Colegio Catolico, Amecameca (1887).

La Aparicion de Santa Maria de Guadalupe by Lic. Primo Feliciano Velazquez. Mexico (1931).

Tres Siglos de Pintura Colonial Mexicana by Agustin Velazquez Chavez. Mexico (1939).

El Gran Acontecimiento Guadalupano by Antonio Pompa y Pompa. Published by Editorial Jus, S.A., Mexico, D.F. (1967).

Descubrimiento de un Busto Humano en los Ojos de la Virgen de Guadalupe by Carlos Salinas and Manuel de la Mora. Published by Editorial Tradicion, Mexico (1980).

Los Ojos de la Virgen de Guadalupe by Dr. Jose Aste` Tonsmann. Published by Editorial Diana, Mexico, D.F. (1981).

Testimonios Historicos Guadalupanos by Ernesto de la Torre Villar & Ramiro Navarro de Anda. Fondo de Cultura Ecomica. Mexico, D.F. (1982).

Forgiving for Health text from **Divine Connections** © 1996 by Cora Hussey.

Harper Collins: Spanish-English Dictionary, 3rd. Edition, San Francisco, CA (1992).

Dorland's Medical Dictionary, 28th Edition. W.B. Saunders Co. Philadelphia, PA (1994).

The Dictionary of Scientific Biography Vol. XI, by Charles Coulston Gillispie. Scribner's Sons New York, New York (1975).

Hirschberg's **History of Ophthalmology**, Vol.7, and Part Two Vol. 11. Bonn (1986).

Dirvy's Spanish-English Dictionary. D.C. Dirvy Inc. Publishers, New York, New York (1945).

Scripture Text: **The New American Bible.** The World Publishing Co. New York, NY (1970).

Bible Quotations: **Roget's Thesaurus of the Bible** by A. Colin Day. Harper Collins Publishers, New York, NY (1992).

BIOGRAPHICAL NOTES

Br. Luis Lasso de la Vega was born in Mexico at the beginning of the XVII century. He had a bachelor's degree from the Royal Pontifical University of Mexico. He was ordained a priest and named chaplain of the Santuary of Guadalupe. In 1646 he wrote in Nahuatl, Huei Tlamahuizoltica Omonoxiti Ilhuicac Tlatoca Ihwapilli Santa Maria, meaning in Spanish, El Gran Acontecimiento Con Que Se Le Aparecio la Senora Santa Reina del Cielo Santa Maria, meaning in English: The Great Event When Our Lady, Holy Mary, Queen of Heanven Made Her Appearance. It was published in Nahuatl and printed in 1649 by Imprenta de Juan Ruyz, under the title of: Totlaconantzin Guadalupe in Nican Huei Altepenahuac Mexico Itocayocan Tepeyacac, meaning in Spanish, El Gran Acontecimiento Con Que Se Le Aparecio La Senora Reina del Cielo Santa Maria, Nuestra Querida Madre de Guadalupe, Aqui Cerca de la Ciudad de Mexico, en un Lugar Nombrado Tepeyacac, meaning in English: The Great Event When Our Lady, Holy Mary of Heaven, Our Dear Mother of Guadalupe, Appeared Here in This City of Mexico, Near a Place called Tepeyac. Then in 1926, Primo Feliciano Velazquez, translated Lasso de la Vega's work into Spanish and published it under the title of Huei Tlamahvicoltica, meaning in Spanish: Se Aparecio Maravillosamente, meaning in English: She Marvelously Appeared. Primo Feliciano Velazquez's work: La Aparicion de Santa Maria de Guadalupe, published in 1931, stemmed from Lasso de la Vega's book: El Gran Acontecimiento, paraphrased and translated into Spanish.

Br. Luis Becerra Tanco was born in 1603 in Taxco, Mexico. He had a bachelor's degree with a major in canonic law. He was ordained a priest, and in 1672 he became a professor of mathematics and astrology at the Universidad de Mexico. Besides Spanish, he spoke Hebrew, Greek, Latin, Italian, French, Portugese, Nahuatl, and Otomi. In 1666 he wrote Origen Milagroso del Santuario de Nuestra Sra. de Guadalupe. After his death in 1672, it was published in 1675 by Dr. Antonio de Gama, with the title of Felicidad de Mexico.

Fr. Francisco de Florencia, S.J., author of La Estrella del Norte de Mexico, was born in Spain in 1620 and died in Mexico in 1695.

Note: Since I am a Latina, I thought it would be amusing to show the reader that not only our names are lengthy, but that we are also wordy when it comes to expressing ourselves. Lasso de la Vega used almost a paragraph for each one of his titles. It was difficult for me to read seventeenth century Spanish during my Guadalupan research, but it was also fun. Now, whenever Hal, my PC, tells me that my sentences are too long, I just tell him: "Mil gracias por recordarme - adelante!" "Thanks for reminding me - go on!" *Cora Hussey*

56

Thank you, my Lady, my Queen, and my Child, for having granted me the honor and the pleasure to write about your apparitions to Juan Diego.

The least of your daughters,

Cora

With Love